Praise for

THE KIDS OF THE POLK STREET SCHOOL

"The stories have a natural air about them. Beginning readers should find themselves easily involved in these 'real' books."   —*Booklist*

"Sims's drawings dance with energy."   —*Publishers Weekly*

Patricia Reilly Giff is the author of many beloved books for children, including the Kids of the Polk Street School books, the Friends and Amigos books, and the Polka Dot Private Eye books.

Several of her novels for older readers have been chosen as ALA Notable books and ALA Best Books for Young Adults. They include *The Gift of the Pirate Queen; All the Way Home; Nory Ryan's Song,* a Society of Children's Book Writers and Illustrators Golden Kite Honor Book for Fiction; *Maggie's Door;* and the Newbery Honor Books *Lily's Crossing* and *Pictures of Hollis Woods. Lily's Crossing* was also chosen as a *Boston Globe–Horn Book* Honor Book. Patricia Reilly Giff's most recent book is *A House of Tailors.* She lives in Connecticut. You can visit her on the Web at www.randomhouse.com/features/patriciareillygiff/.

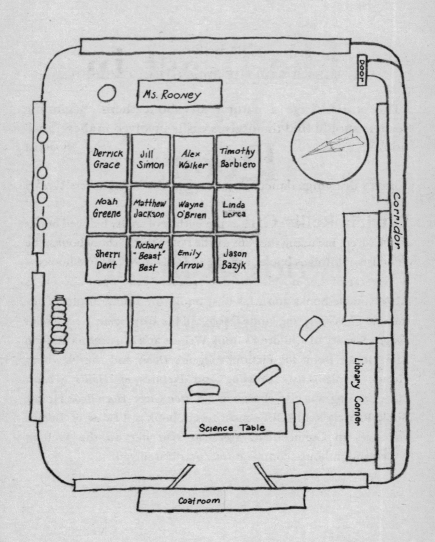

The Beast in Ms. Rooney's Room

Patricia Reilly Giff

Illustrated by Blanche Sims

SCHOLASTIC INC.

New York Toronto London Auckland Sydney
Mexico City New Delhi Hong Kong Buenos Aires

For my mother,
Alice Moeller,
with love

ISBN 0-439-89504-9

Text copyright © 1984 by Patricia Reilly Giff. Illustrations copyright © 1984 by
Blanche Sims. All rights reserved. Published by Scholastic Inc., 557 Broadway, New
York, NY 10012, by arrangement with Random House Children's Books, a division
of Random House, Inc. SCHOLASTIC and associated logos are trademarks
and/or registered trademarks of Scholastic Inc.

12 11 10 9 8 7 6 5 4 3   7 8 9 10 11/0

Printed in the U.S.A.   40

Cover illustration by Joanne Scribner

First Scholastic printing, September 2006

Chapter 1

The nine o'clock bell rang.

Richard Best pounded down the hall of the Polk Street School.

He burst into Room 113.

Ms. Rooney was telling everyone where to sit.

She smiled at Richard and pointed. "Right there behind Matthew Jackson," she said.

Richard slid into the seat behind Matthew. Matthew had stick-out ears and a wet-the-bed smell.

It was September. The first day of school.

Everything was just the same.

The same old classroom, painted up a little.

The same old Ms. Rooney with her puffy brown hair and a lot of orange lip stuff.

There was something different though. The rest of the kids.

Last year they were babies in Mrs. White's class.

1

Now they were in Ms. Rooney's class.

And so was he. Again.

A left-back.

The kids probably thought he was huge. Gigantic. He slid down in his seat. He pulled his head into his neck a little.

A girl sat across from him. She was wearing a pink party dress and dirty red sneakers. Her legs looked like Popsicle sticks.

She had a little white rubber horse on her desk. The kind with a horn on its head. Richard forgot what it was called.

The girl looked over at him and smiled. Maybe she thought he was the one with the wet smell.

He frowned at her. Then he pulled in his breath. Sniffing loudly, he stuck the eraser end of his new pencil up his nose.

He shook his head. The pencil swung back and forth gently.

The girl looked as if she were going to throw up. Good.

Ms. Rooney began to call the roll.

"Emily Arrow," she said.

"Here," said the girl in the party dress and the red sneakers.

Richard tore a piece of paper out of his new notebook. He started to draw a picture of a ship. Then a plane with bombs coming down. Then lots of bullets.

"Timothy Barbiero," Ms. Rooney said.

Richard drew a shark with lots of pointed teeth.

Ms. Rooney said some more names.

Richard put in a sailor jumping over the side of the ship, right into the shark's mouth. "Yee-ouch," he said under his breath.

"Richard Best," Ms. Rooney said.

"Beast," Richard said.

Ms. Rooney looked up. She shook her head.

Matthew turned around. He grinned at Richard.

His teeth were big and curled on the ends.

Richard ran his tongue over his teeth. Little bitty stumpy things.

He pressed on them hard to see if they would wiggle.

4

They didn't.

He was probably the only kid his age in the whole world who still had baby top teeth, Richard thought.

He closed his mouth and clamped his teeth together. He'd have to talk with his mouth almost closed so no one would notice.

He tried to practice under his breath. "I am from outer space," he said without moving his lips.

Ms. Rooney stopped calling the names and looked in his direction.

Richard ducked his head.

"Alex Walker," said Ms. Rooney.

Richard folded his shark picture and put it inside his desk.

He looked out the window while Ms. Rooney called the rest of the names. He wondered what the kids in his old class were doing. His real class.

Maybe he could see them at lunchtime. He'd stay away from these babies. He wouldn't even eat at their table.

He'd tell the old kids he was left back because . . .

Because what?

Ms. Rooney was tapping on her desk with her ruler.

"I'll bet," she said, "we're going to have the banner in Room 113 every week."

The blue banner, Richard thought. Shiny and beautiful. It had a million silky yellow strings hanging down from the bottom.

"Remember," Ms. Rooney said. "You have to be the best class to have the banner."

That's what the banner said in big white letters. BEST.

"The best," Ms. Rooney said again.

Ms. Rooney had said the same things last year, he remembered. He began to dust the top of his table with the little brush on the end of his eraser.

Chapter 2

Richard was hot lunch.

It was Monday. The worst day.

He looked down at his tray: slippery gray chow mein, a dusty kind of peanut butter sandwich, and a paper cup of vanilla ice cream.

He dumped everything off the tray into the garbage pail while the monitor was looking the other way.

Then he changed his mind. He fished around for the ice cream. It had a tan noodle stuck to the top.

He picked the noodle off, licked the top of the ice cream, and ducked out the side door of the cafeteria.

The hall was empty.

No, it wasn't.

At the other end Ms. Rooney was coming around the corner. She had a bunch of yellow and brown paper leaves in her hand. They were probably for the hall bulletin board.

Richard was just passing the boys' room. Quickly he slid inside.

A first-grade boy was washing his hands at the sink.

He looked like a midget, Richard thought.

"Hi," Richard said.

The boy looked as if he were ready to cry.

"Don't cry," Richard said.

The boy didn't answer. He rubbed his wet hands on the sides of his pants.

"I used to be afraid too," Richard said. "When I was in first grade." He glanced out the window to see if any of the kids in his old class were outside yet. "That was a long time ago," he added.

The boy nodded. "What grade are you in?"

"Uh . . . fourth," Richard said, lying.

"Wow," the kid said. He circled around Richard and started for the hall.

"Hey. Wait a minute. What's your name?" Richard called after him.

8

But by that time the kid had raced into the hall. He must have bumped right into Ms. Rooney.

Richard heard a loud oof.

"Slow down, young man," Ms. Rooney said. "Did I hear you talking to someone in there? It sounded like—"

"A fourth-grader," the kid said.

Richard ducked into one of the stalls and closed the door. He waited a few minutes, then he stuck his head out.

Ms. Rooney was probably gone by now, he thought.

He could hear some noise on the playground. It was time to go outside.

He stopped to look in the mirror. He made his eyes cross and stuck out his front teeth. "I am the beast," he said. "The beast with the baby teeth."

He bent down and slurped up some water from the dripping faucet.

Richard dashed out of the boys' room.

Emily Something, the girl in the party dress, was walking along ahead of him.

9

He gave her a little poke.

She twirled around to see who it was.

Richard grinned, trying not to show his teeth.

She kicked out with one of her dirty red sneakers and just missed his shin.

He jumped back. "Hey. Cut it out."

She screwed up her eyes into little slits. "Stay away from me," she said, "or I'll nail you. My father's a cop."

Richard backed away. He made believe he was looking at the yellow-and-brown leaves on the bulletin board.

He waited until Emily was gone.

Then he measured the steps with his eyes. He tried to take them two at a time.

It didn't work.

He tripped a little, stopped to rub his knee, then slowly walked outside.

The kids in his old class were running around on the baseball field, getting ready to play.

He trotted over to them.

"I've got first base," he yelled.

11

"You've got nothing," Drake Evans yelled. "I've got first base."

"I called it first," Richard said. He moved over to stand next to the base.

Drake came charging over. So did a couple of the other kids.

"No left-backs," Drake said.

"Hurry up," said Andrew Bock. He tossed a ball into the air.

Richard looked at the kids. "I called it first," he said again.

Kevin Klein shook his head. "You're not in our class anymore." He looked as if he felt sorry for Richard.

"By a mistake," Richard said. "By accident."

"By dumbness," Drake said. He moved around Richard and stood on the first-base bag.

Richard wanted to push Drake off first. But Drake looked different this year.

Kind of fat. And big. With muscles.

Kevin shook his head again. "Sorry, Richard," he said. "Maybe you'll get skipped next year."

"Listen," Richard said. "I'll tell you why I was left back. Ms. Rooney made a big mistake. She mixed up all the marks."

"Are you sure?" Kevin asked.

Richard nodded slowly. "Someone is very lucky," he said in a loud voice. He stared at Drake Evans. "Someone better watch out that Ms. Rooney doesn't unmix her records."

Drake shoved Richard on the arm. "I don't believe you."

"Yeah," Andrew said. "Richard's making that up."

Richard rubbed his arm a little. It probably would be black and blue by this afternoon. "Someone else should have been left back instead," he yelled.

But no one was paying attention to him now. Except for Kevin.

Kevin licked his lips. "Are you sure?" he asked Richard.

Before Richard could answer, about four kids began to yell at him to get off the field.

Slowly Richard walked away.

He wished he had never started that whole story.

Not only was he a left-back. Now he was a left-back liar.

Chapter 3

It was Monday again, a rainy day.

Richard tried to wiggle his feet around in his sneakers. His socks were still wet from a puddle he had stamped on. His toes felt as if they were stuck together.

The classroom door opened. Someone came in. Someone Richard had never seen before. She was tall and skinny. She had grayish skin the color of Emily Arrow's jump rope, and her eyeglasses were stuck up on her grayish hair.

She was probably about eighty years old, Richard thought.

"My name is Mrs. Paris," she said. "I've just come from another school. I'm the new reading teacher."

Ms. Rooney stopped writing the boardwork. She put down her chalk.

"I have good news for you," Mrs. Paris said.

15

"I'm going to take a few children for reading every day. Extra help for those who are having trouble."

Richard scrunched down in his seat. He could read about ten words.

He'd probably be grown-up before he got into a book with a hard cover on it, he thought.

Ms. Rooney pushed at her puffy brown hair and looked around the room. "That's wonderful," she said.

Richard scrunched down a little further. He stared at Matthew's neck.

Ms. Rooney pointed. "Take Matthew."

Matthew slammed his notebook into his desk.

Too bad for Matthew, Richard thought.

"Alex Walker," said Ms. Rooney. "And Emily Arrow."

Emily Arrow.

Richard couldn't believe it. He thought Emily was the smartest kid in the class.

Emily could add up numbers as fast as anything.

But Ms. Rooney hadn't started reading groups yet. Richard hadn't heard Emily read.

16

She was probably terrible. Worse than he was. Good. Terrific.

"I think that's all," Ms. Rooney was saying to Mrs. Paris.

Richard shoved his tongue against his top tooth. It was still stuck in his gum like a little piece of cement.

So what? He didn't have to go to reading.

"Come, children," Mrs. Paris said. "We'll go down to the Reading Room."

"Wait a minute," Ms. Rooney said. "I think I forgot someone."

Richard didn't even wait to hear his name called. He pushed his notebook inside his desk.

"I don't know how I could have forgotten Richard," said Ms. Rooney. "Richard Best."

"Richard Worst," Emily said.

They followed Mrs. Paris down the hall. The Reading Room was full of junk.

The pictures on the bulletin board were left over from last spring, when the other reading teacher was there. There were dirty-looking bunnies with cotton-puff tails, and tulips that didn't have any color left.

All the windows were closed and the shades were down.

"It smells in here," Matthew said.

Richard was surprised that Matthew could smell anything. "Like what?" he asked.

Matthew raised his shoulders up in the air. "Sauerkraut, I think. Or asparagus."

"Smells like someone wet the bed," Alex Walker said.

Mrs. Paris poked at her eyeglasses.

"Just take everything off the chairs," she said.

She went over to the windows, opened one a little, and began to snap up the shades.

Richard slid into a seat at the big round table. Alex sat down on one side of him and Matthew on the other.

Emily sat across from him. He tried not to look at her.

There was a pile of drawing paper in the middle of the table. He reached for the top piece.

He'd draw a picture of his mother. He'd make her standing in the kitchen on her day off from Penney's department store. He'd put his sister, Holly, in too.

By this time Mrs. Paris was finished with the windows. She dragged another chair to the table.

"Now," she said, and sat down next to Emily Arrow.

Richard added two lines for a neck.

"Time for me to know your names," Mrs. Paris said.

"Matthew."

"Alex."

Mrs. Paris looked at Richard. "How about you?"

"Beast," Richard said. He looked at Mrs. Paris out of the corner of his eye.

Mrs. Paris blinked.

"It is not," Emily said.

"What did you say?" Mrs. Paris asked him.

Richard looked out at the rain. It was smashing into the windowpanes. There was a puddle on the ledge under the open window.

20

"Beast," he said.

Mrs. Paris leaned forward a little. "Did you say beast?" she asked.

Richard raised his shoulders up in the air. His old friend Joseph had called him that. Richard Beast instead of Richard Best.

His old friend from his old class.

Now his old friend had moved away. And his old class was gone too.

Matthew poked at him under the table and grinned a little.

But Richard didn't smile back. Who wanted to be friends with a baby? Especially someone with big dirty ears. Someone who still wet the bed.

Mrs. Paris nodded. "All right," she said. "Beast it is." She looked at Emily. "And what's your name?"

"I'm Emily," Emily said. "Emily Arrow. And that's my *real* name."

Mrs. Paris smiled a little.

Richard almost thought she winked at him.

He drew some more lines on his picture.

21

Mrs. Paris started to pass out some reading books. Skinny little things with covers you could bend in two seconds, Richard thought.

"It's a funny thing about learning," Mrs. Paris said. "Some people zip into reading right away. Some people take a little longer." She smiled at them. "But don't worry. Everybody's good at something."

Richard looked around. He wondered if that was true. Emily was great at adding. He was good at art. He wondered what Matthew was good at. Wetting the bed, maybe.

He opened his baby reader.

There were five words on the first page.

He knew two of them.

He raised his hand. "Can I go to the boys' room?"

Mrs. Paris nodded. "I figured that was what you were going to ask me," she said.

Richard got as far as the door.

"Don't take too long," she said. "I've got a pile of Candy Corn in my desk."

Chapter 4

Two weeks later was assembly. The whole school was going to see a puppet show.

Ms. Rooney made the class sit boy-girl, boy-girl. Somehow Richard got stuck between Emily Arrow and Jill Simon.

Emily stuck her feet up against the back of the seat in front of her. Then she leaned her elbow on the armrest next to Richard.

He moved away a little.

He began to feel his top teeth with his tongue. Maybe he should start wiggling them around, he thought. Maybe he should wiggle them about a hundred times a day.

Loosen them up.

He reached into his mouth.

"Sucking your thumb?" Emily asked.

Richard pulled his fingers out of his mouth.

Mrs. Kettle, the strictest teacher in the whole

school, was walking up and down the aisle. She saw Emily with her feet up. She waved her finger at Emily's red sneakers.

Emily put her feet down. She left her elbow hanging on Richard's side of the seat.

Richard wondered what would happen if he gave her a good punch in the arm.

Instead, he began to push at his teeth with his tongue.

Twenty-five, twenty-six, twenty-seven, he counted to himself.

His tongue began to get tired. But his teeth didn't seem to be moving one little bit.

Behind him there was a lot of noise. He turned around to look.

It was his old class, marching into the auditorium.

Not boy-girl, boy-girl. That was for babies.

No. First there was a line of boys. Then a line of girls.

They marched right into the row behind him.

Quickly he turned his head around again. He looked at the blue curtain in front of the stage.

Mr. Mancina, the principal, turned out the lights.

In front of the auditorium the curtain opened.

A lady came out. "Today we're going to have *Hansel and Gretel*," she said. "I know you're going to love it."

Richard didn't think he was going to love it. He had seen it last year at the library.

It was terrible.

The lady went back inside. Two puppets came floating down from the ceiling.

Hansel and Gretel.

In back of him Richard could hear Drake Evans talking with Kevin Klein.

He wondered if they knew he was sitting right in front of them. He kept his head straight so they couldn't see his face.

He wondered if they knew the back of his neck.

Hansel and Gretel were sprinkling bread crumbs all over the stage.

They were yelling as they sprinkled.

After a while Richard's neck started to feel stiff from keeping it so straight.

He was afraid to rub it.

Maybe they knew what his hand looked like.

He wished he had a pencil and a piece of paper. He wished he could draw a picture. He'd draw a picture of Saturday, when his father was home all day.

Drake and Kevin were laughing.

Maybe they were laughing at him.

Suddenly Emily turned around. "Shh," she hissed at them.

Richard slid down in his seat.

For a moment Drake and Kevin were quiet.

Then Drake said, "Don't talk, Kevin. The babies want to watch *Hansel and Gretel*."

Richard gulped.

"Richard wants to watch *Hansel and Gretel*," Drake said. "Don't you?"

Richard stared at the stage. His mouth felt dry.

Emily put her feet up on the seat in front of her again.

Richard felt Drake giving him a little poke in the back. "Right, Richard?" Drake asked.

26

Up on the stage the witch was putting Hansel into some kind of cage thing. "Ha, ha, ha," she was saying in a scratchy old voice.

"Richard likes this baby puppet show," Drake said.

Richard swiveled around. He was going to hit Drake Evans. He was going to—

His elbow caught Emily's arm. Hard.

"Ouch," she said.

"Who is that?" Mrs. Kettle whispered in a loud voice. She poked her head into Richard's aisle. "Is that you, Emily?"

Emily ducked her head.

"Get out here," Mrs. Kettle said. "Stand against the wall."

Slowly Emily stood up. Her face was all red.

It's my fault, Richard wanted to say. But all the kids in his old class were sitting right there, looking at them.

Emily didn't say anything. She squeezed past him. She marched over to the wall.

She looked as if she wanted to cry.

But she didn't cry. She took her white rubber horse with the horn out of her pocket and held it in her hand.

Emily was tough.

Tougher than he was.

Up on the stage Gretel was dancing around.

Richard sighed. He wished it were summertime again. He wished he were fishing with his father.

He wished at least it were Saturday.

Chapter 5

Richard raised his hand.

Ms. Rooney was writing something up at her desk. She didn't look up.

He wiggled his hand around a little.

"Ms. Rooney," he called in a loud whisper.

She looked up and frowned. "You're supposed to raise your hand," she said.

"Can I sharpen my pencil?"

"How many times have you sharpened that pencil today?"

"There's one spot of wood on the pencil. I can't write with that side," he said.

"How many times?" Ms. Rooney asked.

"Three, I think."

"Four," said Sherri Dent from the desk next to Richard.

"This is the last time," said Ms. Rooney.

Richard went up to the pencil sharpener. He

stood there for a long time, looking out the window. It was a great day outside. Great for football.

Slowly he went back to his seat. He copied the last sentence of his boardwork.

It was a letter. A long one. Everyone in the class had to copy a thank-you to the P.T.A. for the puppet show they had seen the other day.

He put down his pencil and rubbed the side of his middle finger.

Then he looked at his letter. It was kind of a mess. Some parts were dark and some parts were light.

His pencil was terrible.

He looked up at the clock. The little hand was on the ten. The big hand was on the five.

Almost time for reading with Mrs. Paris.

He reached into his desk. He pulled out the pictures he had cut out of an old magazine the night before.

Pictures of things with short *a*'s in them.

An apple. A turkey with some cranberry sauce next to it.

Cranberry. Craaan, he whispered to himself.

Right. He drew a circle around the cranberry sauce with his pencil.

A picture of a star. A cat eating from a bowl of cereal. A baby.

Baby. Baaaby. He looked at the picture for a second. No. He crumpled it up and shoved it back in his desk.

"Time for reading," Ms. Rooney said.

Now he had only four pictures. He was supposed to have five.

If only he had brought the magazine with him. He could see it. Right on the hall table.

Ms. Rooney had a bunch of magazines on the shelf in the corner. Maybe he could—

"Reading," Ms. Rooney said again.

Richard stood up. He followed Matthew up the aisle. Then he darted over to the shelf and reached for the magazine.

Ms. Rooney sighed. "Richard," she said. "Put that down. Mrs. Paris is waiting."

Richard looked at the magazine for a moment.

There was a picture of a girl in a hat right on the front cover.

It was perfect.

"Richard . . ." Ms. Rooney began.

Richard put the magazine back in the pile. He raced out of the room after the rest of the kids.

He made sure he stayed behind Emily Arrow. He had tried not to look at her all morning. He didn't like to think about what had happened in the auditorium yesterday.

He wondered if Emily felt bad.

He wondered if she had told her father.

He passed the fifth-grade room. Holly's class. He went back and looked in the little window in the door. Holly's head was bent over her desk.

Her friend Joanne was sitting in front of her.

Up in the front of the classroom was the blue banner. Holly's class had won it for the week.

Lucky.

He caught up with Matthew just as they opened the door to Mrs. Paris's room.

Mrs. Paris was sitting at the table waiting for them.

He reached for a piece of drawing paper from the pile in the middle of the table.

While Emily was telling Mrs. Paris about what she wanted to be when she grew up, Richard tried to think of something interesting with an *a* in it. A short *a*. Something better than a hat. Something he could draw.

"You know," Emily said. "A person who does somersaults. On a mat. In the Olympics." She smiled. "Or maybe a runner. Like Uni." She held up her rubber animal. "My unicorn."

Richard bent his head over the paper and began to draw.

"Well, now," Mrs. Paris said. She reached into the drawer under the table. "Dried figs," she said. She put a bunch of them on the table in front of her. "Help yourself."

They were little brown rolled-up things.

They probably tasted horrible.

Ordinarily Richard wouldn't have tried them.

34

But the morning was only half over, and he hadn't finished his cereal at breakfast.

He stuck a fig in his mouth and tried to chew it without tasting it.

"Who wants to show us a picture of short *a*?" Mrs. Paris asked, her mouth full of fig.

Matthew held up a picture of an apple.

It was just like Richard's.

Matthew's mother probably got the same magazines as his mother.

Emily held up a picture of a cat.

Richard held up his picture of a star.

"Ah," said Mrs. Paris. "Not exactly."

"Bossy *r*," said Emily in a loud voice.

"Right, Emily," Mrs. Paris said.

Bossy *r*, Richard thought. What was that all about? It sounded familiar somehow. He looked at Emily out of the corner of his eye.

"Bossy *r*," said Emily, "means that *r* changes the sound of the *a*. It doesn't sound like *a*, apple. It just sounds like *r*. Ar, star." She raised her shoulders up in the air.

"Park," said Alex.

"Terrific," Mrs. Paris said. "Got it, Richard?"

Richard nodded. "I remember now."

"It's all right to forget," Mrs. Paris said. "I still haven't remembered to clean this room."

Richard looked around. She was right. The room was still in a big mess. The bunnies and tulips were gone but the same old blue paper covered the bulletin board. It had five dark spots where the tulips and bunnies had been.

Mrs. Paris was looking at the rest of the pictures. All of them except the picture Richard had drawn.

Maybe she hadn't been counting. Maybe she didn't know that he had only four pictures and everyone else had five. Maybe she wouldn't ask.

But then he looked down at his drawing. He liked it.

He pushed it across the table. "I drew this," he said.

"Neat," said Mrs. Paris. "Really neat."

Emily looked over Mrs. Paris's shoulder. "It's an—" She stopped and grinned.

Matthew leaned across the table. "An arrow."

"Aaaarrow. Emily Arrow," Richard said. For the first time he looked at Emily. "It has an *r*. But it's not a bossy one."

Mrs. Paris smiled. "There's always something to mix people up, isn't there? It's called an exception to the rule."

Mrs. Paris held up his picture. "Let's hang this up. We'll stick it right in the middle of the bulletin board." She reached back on her desk and handed Richard a thumbtack. "Go ahead."

Richard marched up to the bulletin board. He stuck the arrow up over one of the dark spots.

The arrow looked good. But the rest of the bulletin board looked terrible.

Chapter 6

Richard hated Thursdays.

His mother worked late and he had to walk home with his big sister, Holly.

She and her friend Joanne were always the last ones out.

Richard waited on the stone steps in front of the school.

He watched some ants come out of a little hole in the middle step. They headed for someone's leftover cookie on the bottom step.

After a few minutes there were about a hundred ants rushing back and forth.

He built a little stick bridge to help them out.

One of the ants spotted it and climbed up. After a few minutes they were all marching along on the stick.

Richard stood up and peered through the window into the hall.

Holly and Joanne were all the way down the other end. They were talking and laughing and acting as if they'd be an hour just walking down one hall.

They didn't care that he had to waste his whole afternoon waiting for them.

He went back and watched the ants.

At last Holly and Joanne opened the door. They started down the path. Richard jumped off the steps and followed them.

They went down Cole Street. Instead of crossing at the corner, they turned in at the big doors of the library.

"Got to get a book for a book report," Holly called over her shoulder. "A book report on James K. Polk."

Richard caught up with them. "Who?" he asked as they opened the doors.

"Polk," Holly said again.

"Who's that?"

"He doesn't know anything," Holly told Joanne.

"I do so."

"It's a president," Joanne said.

40

"Don't you even know the name of your school?" Holly asked.

"Polk Street," Richard said. "That's a president's name?" He shook his head. "He's got a funny first name."

Holly started to laugh. She leaned against Joanne. "I told you, Joanne," she said after a minute. "He's a dummy."

"Not Polk Street," Joanne said. "The school is *on* Polk Street. They're both named for President Polk. President James K. Polk."

"Don't try to tell him," Holly said. "He doesn't even know George Washington."

"I do so," Richard said.

"Or Christopher Columbus."

"I do so."

"Who was he?"

Richard stopped. "A president."

Holly and Joanne went over to one of the tables. "Dumb," Holly said.

"I remember now," Richard said. He felt like clipping Holly right on her frizzy brown hair. "I remember the whole thing. Christopher Columbus discovered America. He had three boats. I even know their names.''

But they weren't paying any attention.

He went to the back to look for his favorite book. The one with the red cover and all the pictures.

Last time he was there, he had hidden it.

He knelt down next to one of the racks. He looked on the bottom shelf.

It wasn't there.

It was gone. He wondered if he'd ever find it again.

He stood up. He bumped right into Drake Evans.

''What are you doing here?'' Drake asked.

''Reading.'' Richard stepped around him. He pretended to be looking for a book.

''Reading what?'' Drake asked.

''Watch out,'' Richard said over his shoulder. ''I saw Ms. Rooney checking over her marking book yesterday.''

Drake followed him down the aisle. ''You're lying, Richard,'' he said.

Richard pulled a book off the shelf. It was a fat one. Huge.

He opened it up and made believe he was reading it.

"You can't read that," Drake said.

"I can so."

Drake started to laugh. "You have to go to remedial reading."

"Special," Richard said. "Special reading."

"Because you can't read. Baby."

Baby. Richard pushed at his teeth with his tongue.

"That's not true," he said, keeping his top lip down as far as he could.

Drake started to walk away.

"It's special reading for the smart kids," Richard said.

Drake looked back. "Kids who wet the bed," he said. "Like your friend Matthew."

"He's not my friend," Richard said. He wondered how Drake knew so much about everything.

Drake laughed again. "He's your friend, all right. He told me. And you both go to baby reading."

Richard looked down at his book. "I have to do a report," he said. "That's why I'm reading this book. I have to do a report on—"

"On kindergarten stuff," Drake said.

"No," Richard said. "On James K. Polk. I bet you don't even know who that is."

Drake pushed him. "You just made him up. There's no such person."

"I knew it," Richard said. "That's why Mr. Mancina told me to—"

"To what?"

"To find out who the dumb kids are. To see who should have been left back instead of me. The kids who bother everyone. The kids who don't even know that James K. Polk was a president."

"Liar."

"Besides," said Richard, "Mr. Mancina said we were going to get the banner. Just because of me. Just because—"

He closed his mouth. He couldn't think of anything else to say.

He backed down the aisle with Drake still looking at him.

"Hey," a voice said from in back of the magazine rack. "Beast."

He twirled around.

It was Emily Arrow. She was sitting on the floor paging through a book.

"Hi," he said. He wondered if she had heard him talking to Drake. He wondered if she had told her father that she had to stand against the wall all because of him.

"Did you say we're going to get the banner?" she asked.

He looked back down the aisle. Drake was gone.

"Uh. Well," he said. He went over to the magazine rack. "I meant to tell you." He swallowed. "I'm sorry."

"About the wall?" She pulled the horse with the horn out of her pocket. "It's all right. I'm tough. I've got my unicorn." She galloped him across her book. "He makes me tough."

"I know you're tough," Richard said.

"Mr. Mancina told you we were going to get the banner?"

He sank down on the floor next to her. "No, I made it up."

"Let's try for it," Emily said.

"How?"

"I don't know." Emily shook her head.

Richard looked up at the front desk. Drake was checking out some books. Three or four. Big ones with hard covers.

"I wish we could," Richard said.

"Come on, Richard," Holly called from the front.

"I have to go now," he said.

Emily's head was bent over her book. "I wish I could read this," she said, "instead of looking at all the pictures."

Richard didn't say anything. He followed Holly out the door. He turned back to wave at Emily before he shut the door behind him.

Chapter 7

Richard was in early the next morning.

There were only about six kids in the classroom.

Emily Arrow was sitting on top of her desk. She was showing Ms. Rooney her white unicorn.

Alex was watering the plants.

Sherri Dent was telling Alex to stop spilling water on the floor.

Wayne was standing at the science table in the back. He was the shortest kid in the class and had the biggest teeth. He was dropping tiny dots of powdered food into the fishbowl he had brought in the other day.

Everyone said hi to Richard.

"You're early," Emily said.

Richard ducked his head.

"We were talking yesterday," Emily Arrow said to Ms. Rooney. "Beast and me. We were talking about winning the banner."

"Good for you," Ms. Rooney said. She turned her head for a moment and smiled. Then she went back to writing the new spelling words on the blackboard.

Richard walked over to the back table to look at the fishbowl. There were two fish swimming around inside. He knocked on the glass a little to see if they would pay any attention to him.

They didn't. Maybe they were too busy eating their food to think about what was going on in the classroom.

"What are their names?" Richard asked Wayne.

"The striped one is Harry," he said. "The other one doesn't have a name yet."

"How come?" Richard asked.

"He's mean," Wayne said. "He hogs all the food. I can't think of a mean name for him."

"I know a mean name," Richard said.

"What?"

"Drake."

"Like that big kid?" Wayne asked. "The one in your old class?"

"Just like him," Richard said.

Wayne looked at the fish for a moment. "I guess he looks like a Drake. All right." He called up to Ms. Rooney. "Richard just named my fish."

Ms. Rooney turned around again to look at them. "What's his name?"

"Drake," Wayne said.

"Drake?" Ms. Rooney asked. "That's a nice name."

Richard and Wayne grinned at each other.

Emily came back to watch the fish. "Hey, Harry," she said. She tapped on the side of the bowl.

"You want to win the banner?" Wayne asked.

Richard nodded.

"How?"

"That's what we don't know," Emily said.

Ms. Rooney finished with the boardwork. She put down her chalk and walked to the back of the room.

"We don't know how to win the banner," Emily said.

51

"By doing the best you can," Ms. Rooney said.

"But suppose no one notices?" Emily asked.

Ms. Rooney raised her eyebrows. "They'll notice, all right. Be good in the hall. Don't get in trouble at recess." She stopped for a second. "Or in the boys' room."

Richard wondered if she was looking at him.

"We can tell the rest of the kids too," Emily said.

"Right," Richard agreed. He went back to his desk. He couldn't remember what his mother had given him for lunch.

It was tuna fish. He could smell it right through the bag.

Matthew slid into the seat in front of him.

Matthew had wet the bed again.

He smelled a little bit like the tuna fish.

Richard opened the bag to see if there was any dessert.

Cookies.

The terrible kind with the orange-tasting stuff in the middle.

"What have you got for lunch?" Matthew asked him.

"Tuna fish."

"I've got Fluffernutter," Matthew said.

"What?"

"Peanut butter and marshmallow. My mother put it on rye bread. It's the best."

Richard thought it was probably the best too. "Lucky," he said.

"Want some?" Matthew asked.

Richard could taste it in his mouth. Gooey. Peanut-buttery. Rye-bready.

If only Matthew didn't wet the bed.

He shook his head. "I like tuna fish."

Matthew looked a little disappointed. Maybe he didn't like Fluffernutter as much as he said he did, Richard thought. Maybe he was dying for some of Richard's tuna fish. No, Richard told himself, it was because Matthew wanted to share. Matthew wanted to be friends.

But Richard didn't even want to touch Matthew's lunch bag. "Want some of my tuna fish?" he asked.

"Naah," Matthew said. He turned around and started to copy his spelling.

Richard hoped Matthew's feelings weren't hurt. He hoped Matthew didn't guess why he didn't want to share his Fluffernutter.

By this time everyone was in the classroom. Everyone but Emily's friend Jill. She had been coughing a lot yesterday. She was probably home in bed. Sick. Watching television. Having a snack on a tray.

Maybe Fluffernutter.

Ms. Rooney held up her hand. "Emily Arrow wants to say something," she said.

Emily marched up to the front of the room.

"We want to win the banner, right?" Emily said to the class.

Nobody said anything. They were all busy with their boardwork, or sharpening their pencils, or looking out the window.

54

"Hey," Emily yelled. "Pay attention."

"That's right," Ms. Rooney said. "Wait a minute, Emily. We'll wait for everyone to listen."

At last everyone was quiet.

"Beast wants to win the banner," Emily said. "And me too. And Wayne."

"Who's Beast?" Noah Greene asked.

Emily made a face as if Noah were crazy. "Richard Best, of course. You didn't know that's his nickname?"

Noah looked embarrassed. He turned around and smiled a little at Richard.

"So everyone be good," Emily said.

"Especially in the halls," Wayne said.

"And in the boys' room," Richard said.

"Everywhere," Matthew said.

Mrs. Paris stuck her head in the door. "Reading. All right?" she asked Ms. Rooney. "I have to go to a meeting later. May I take the children now?"

"Certainly," Ms. Rooney said. "I hope they're working hard in reading."

"I'll tell you something," Mrs. Paris said. "They're terrific. Top kids."

Richard grinned at Emily. That Mrs. Paris was much nicer than she had looked in the beginning.

He stood up and followed Matthew out the door. He was going to walk down the hall as quietly as he could.

Winning the banner was going to be easy. He knew it.

Chapter 8

It was time for gym. Richard tied his sneakers a little tighter. He hitched up his gym shorts.

Mr. Bell, the gym teacher, was waiting for them. He tossed a basketball to Alex Walker.

For a moment Alex stood there watching them. Then he threw the ball at Matthew.

Matthew ducked. Then they were all running. And yelling. Trying to stay away from Alex and the ball. It was a terrific game.

Richard saw Alex coming toward him. He tried to get out of the way, but he tripped. He skidded down onto the shiny gym floor.

"Look at Beast," Emily called. "He's bleeding."

Richard stood up and looked at his leg. There was a round red circle in the middle of his knee.

Everyone came running over.

"Why don't you go down to the nurse," Mr. Bell said. "Get a bandage."

Richard didn't know what to do. He hated to miss gym. But he liked going to see Mrs. Ames, the nurse.

Everyone did.

She had plaid bandages and raisins.

"All right," he said. "I'll be right back."

He hurried down to the nurse's office. There was a bunch of kids ahead of him.

One boy was sitting on the cot. The thermometer paper was stuck to his forehead. A first-grader was leaning on the chair next to Mrs. Ames's desk.

Mrs. Ames was in the little room next to this one. Richard could hear her talking on the phone. She was telling a mother to come to school to pick up a sick kid.

Richard looked at the first-grader. He wondered if he was going to throw up.

Richard moved away from him. He went over near the window. While he was waiting he thought about the banner. Everyone in the class was trying to win.

Nobody ran in the hall.

Nobody had gotten into trouble all week.

Richard couldn't wait until Mr. Mancina told them who won. He was sure it would be his class.

He stood there waiting a long time. Mrs. Ames stopped talking on the phone. She put ice on a boy's wrist.

Richard looked at his knee. It had stopped bleeding.

Maybe he should go back to gym.

But what about the bandage? And the raisins?

The window was open a little. It smelled good outside.

He stuck his hand out. Then he bent his head down so he could breathe some of the nice air.

There were people outside. Mothers with baby carriages. Three little kids were running back and forth across the school lawn.

Richard wondered what they'd think if they saw something fly out the window.

Something like a plane.

He spotted some white paper on the nurse's desk. He reached for a piece.

Quickly he folded it into a plane. He couldn't wait to see what the kids would do. Maybe they wouldn't see it come from the window. Maybe they'd think it came from somewhere else.

Somewhere far away. Outer space.

He shot it out the window.

It sailed a little bit. Then it settled down on the school lawn.

No one even saw it. One of the kids ran right over it.

Richard reached for another paper and sailed it out the window.

This time a little girl spotted it. She ran to get it.

Richard thought he'd make another one. Maybe two. One for each kid. He'd sail them out the window together. Use both hands.

He opened the window a little more. Then he took the new planes, one in each hand, and—

"What are you doing?" said a voice. "Just what is going on?"

It was Mrs. Ames. She looked cranky.

Before Richard had time to answer, she said,

"Richard Best. Go back to your classroom. I'm going to report you to your teacher. And to Mr. Mancina."

Richard threw the planes in the wastebasket. Slowly he walked back to the gym. He wondered what everyone would think when they saw him without a bandage. Without any raisins.

He wondered what everyone would say when they heard that he had been reported.

His class had just lost the banner for the week. And it was all his fault.

Chapter 9

Richard was right. The second grade didn't win the banner. The next day Mr. Mancina told them over the loudspeaker that Mrs. Kettle's class had won.

For a couple of days Richard didn't tell anyone it was his fault.

On Thursday, just before spelling, he told Emily.

For a minute Emily looked as if she were going to get mad. But then she raised her shoulders in the air. "Don't worry," she said. "We'll get it next time."

But she didn't look as if she really believed it.

And Richard didn't either. He was always doing something wrong.

Today they were having spelling partners. It was just his luck that Matthew was his spelling partner. Matthew sat down at his desk, practically on top of him.

"Only ten minutes to study together," Ms. Rooney called from the front of the room. "The test is in ten . . . no, nine minutes from now."

"Spelling is easy," Matthew said. He grinned at Richard and shuffled through the pages of the spelling book. "Here it is, lesson four."

Richard inched his chair away from Matthew a little. He looked down at the ten spelling words for lesson four.

He hated spelling.

Last night his mother made Holly go over all his spelling words with him.

Holly didn't ask the words one-two-three the way he wanted her to. She skipped around and mixed him all up.

Then she got mad when he made mistakes.

"Spelling is easy," Matthew said again. "All you have to do is stick some little words together. Turn them into big ones."

"Like what?"

Matthew scratched at his ear. "Like what? Let me see. Like Noah."

"Noah?"

"You know—Noah." Matthew pointed to the seat next to his. "By the window."

Richard nodded. "What about him?"

"Do you know how to spell his name?"

Richard shook his head. "No."

"Easy," Matthew said. "You know how to spell *no*?"

"Everybody knows how to—"

"Do you know how to spell *a*?"

Richard nodded again.

"Stick them together," Matthew said. "Go ahead."

"No, a," Richard said. "N-o-a," he spelled out loud. "Hey. You're right."

"It's time to put your spellers away now," Ms. Rooney said. "Take out a piece of white paper."

Matthew went back to his seat. Richard took out his looseleaf book.

All the pages looked a little crumpled. Most of them had drawings all over them.

He pulled out a piece and looked at the picture he had drawn the other day.

It was a picture of Holly. She was holding their cat, Meow. They were both smiling.

He reached for his pink eraser.

"Put your name on top," Ms. Rooney said.

He began to erase the picture so he could use the paper for the test.

He went a little too hard. Suddenly there was a hole in the paper. Right on top of Meow.

"Meow," Richard said under his breath. "Me. Ow." He wrote his name in while he was waiting for Ms. Rooney to say the first word. M-e, he spelled in his head. O-w. He looked at Matthew and nodded. "Meow."

"Who is making cat noises back there?" Ms. Rooney asked.

Why hadn't anyone told him about spelling before? he wondered. It was easy.

"First word," Ms. Rooney said. "Along."

Along. With his thumb Richard tried to flatten out the hole he had made in his paper.

Easy. A. Long. Along.

"Could," Ms. Rooney said.

Richard pushed at his teeth. Could. He tried to say it slowly. To find the little words inside.

There weren't any.

It was just could.

He remembered Holly yelling at him last night. Was it *c*? Or *k*?

He knew there was an *l*.

C-u-l-d.

It didn't look right.

Too bad it didn't work out the way Matthew said. It was probably one of those things Mrs. Paris had said. An exception.

"Backyard," Ms. Rooney said.

In front of him Matthew muttered, "Back . . . yard."

Richard looked at Matthew's ears. Back. Yard. Easy. With a bossy *r*. Easy as anything.

68

Matthew was right. That baby with the wet-the-bed smell was right.

He wasn't such a baby.

He wondered if Matthew hated to wet the bed.

Just the way he hated his little baby front teeth.

He gave Matthew a little punch on the back. Then quickly he began to spell backyard.

Chapter 10

Today was banner day: the day Mr. Mancina would tell them who won.

Richard's class had tried hard this week.

Even if they didn't win the banner, they were the best. He knew it.

"Time for reading," Ms. Rooney said.

Quietly they started down the hall.

Kevin Klein was coming out of the boys' room.

"Hi," Richard said. He remembered to whisper. "I've been meaning to tell you. Ms. Rooney didn't really mix her records up."

"Whew," Kevin said. "I was really worried. I thought it was me."

"It takes some people a little time to zip into reading," Richard said. "That's what happened to me."

Kevin nodded slowly. "You're a good artist though."

"Right," Richard said. "That's right."

He started down the hall and looked back over his shoulder. "Are you going to tell Drake?"

"That kid can find out for himself," Kevin said. "Let him ask the teacher if he wants to know."

They grinned at each other. Then Richard rushed down the hall to reading.

He didn't remember the surprise in his desk until he was almost at Mrs. Paris's door.

"I forgot something," he told Mrs. Paris. "Can I go back to my room for a minute?"

"Sure," Mrs. Paris said. "But try not to take an hour."

Richard shook his head. He wanted to get back to reading. Even though they were reading a little skinny baby book, it was kind of interesting. It was all about a kid who got lost in a snowstorm.

Besides, he was beginning to know a lot of the words. Not all of them. But a lot more than he ever thought he would.

He started to race down the hall. But then he remembered the banner.

He slowed down.

He made believe he was caught in the snowstorm. He closed his eyes and took about ten steps.

But then he remembered the banner.

He opened his eyes and hurried into his classroom.

"Forgot something," he told Ms. Rooney.

Richard raced back to his desk. He pulled out his notebook and went into the hall again.

He stopped at Holly's classroom to wave to her, then bent over the faucet for a quick drink.

A very quick drink. He didn't want to get into trouble for hanging around in the hall.

Drake was coming out of the boys' room.

"Hey, Richard."

Richard turned around. "Shh," he said. He could see Mrs. Kettle at the other end of the hall.

Richard started to walk down the hall as fast as he could without running.

Drake followed him. He was banging on the wall with a wooden pass.

Mrs. Kettle started down the hall toward them. She was frowning.

Richard ducked into Room 100 just in time.

He looked at Mrs. Paris. And Emily and the other two kids. They were waiting for him.

He opened his notebook and pulled out the surprises.

He had worked on them until bedtime the night before.

"I made some drawings for the bulletin board," he said.

Everyone looked up.

"To cover the spots," he said. "The bunny spots and the tulip spots."

Mrs. Paris reached for his drawings. She looked at them carefully. "You're a great kid," she said. "The best."

There was a noise. The loudspeaker.

Emily looked at him. Then she covered her eyes. "It's Mr. Mancina," she said. "Cross your fingers. Cross your toes."

Richard crossed his fingers. So did everyone else.

"I have good news," Mr. Mancina said.

He said that every time he announced the winner.

Richard looked at Matthew. Matthew grinned at him. "I hope it's us," he said.

"Ms. Rooney's class," Mr. Mancina said.

Emily Arrow yelled. So did Alex. And Matthew. So did he.

They could hear the rest of their class yelling in Ms. Rooney's room.

Ms. Rooney had promised them a party if they won. Cookies and juice.

It was going to be a great day.

Mrs. Paris handed Richard some thumbtacks. He went over to the bulletin board. Carefully, while the rest of them watched, he tacked up his pictures.

He had made a big fat bossy *r* sitting on a squished little *a*. He had drawn a dark brown Alex and a Matthew with ears. He had drawn a Mrs. Paris with glasses. She was smiling at an Emily Arrow and her unicorn.

And last he had drawn himself. He had a book in his hand. Not a big fat book. But not a little skinny book either. Kind of an in-between book.

He went back to his seat. He wanted to find out what had happened to the kid in the snowstorm.

He paged through the book to find his place. At the same time he pushed at his teeth.

''Hey,'' he said.

Everyone looked at him.

He didn't want to tell them that one of his teeth was wiggling.

Not much. But a little.

''Can I read first?'' he asked, and grinned.